MW01138762

Also by Amelia Littlewood
Death at the Netherfield Park Ball
The Mystery of the Indian Diadem
The Peculiar Doctor Barnabus
The Apparition at Rosing's Park
The Shadow of Moriarty
The Adventure of the King's Portrait

ISBN: 9781973222965

FROM THE JANE AUSTEN NOVEL
Pride & Prejudice

DEATH
AT THE
NETHERFIELD
PARK BALL

A Sherlock Holmes & Elizabeth Bennet Mystery

AMELIA LITTLEWOOD

CYANIDE PUBLISHING

Chapter One:
The Mysterious Mr. Bingley

It is a truth universally acknowledged, that a single man in possession of a good fortune, must be in want of a wife. Or so I thought. My opinion forever changed the day I met a very peculiar man by the name of Mr. Sherlock Holmes.

~~ o ~~

"Did you hear?" Mrs. Bennet said, looking up from her needlework. When Mr. Bennet did not respond, she asked again. "Mr. Bennet, *my dear*, have you heard the news?"

After some time, Mr. Bennet looked up from his book. "My dear Mrs. Bennet, I have heard much news today. To which bit of it are you referring?"

"Why, the news that Netherfield Park has been let at last."

"No, my dear, I had not heard that *particular* piece of news."

Mrs. Bennet looked up from her needlework once more. My darling sister Jane and I shared a humorous glance.

"Do you not want to hear who it has been let out to?" she asked, eagerness in her voice.

"I suppose you will tell me no matter my response," the man replied dryly. He had been a constant companion to my mother's nerves for near three decades. His calm demeanor was the only way he could have survived those long years.

"Why, Mr. Bennet, it has been let by a young man of large fortune!" she exclaimed.

"What is the man's name?"

"Bingley."

"Is he single?" Although our father claimed to be above such nonsense as marrying his daughters off, he asked the question with feigned disinterest.

My youngest sister let out a gasp. She was consumed with the thought of matrimony, and in what she would claim to be love with near every eligible man she crossed paths with. It was unlikely that she would marry before myself and Jane were wed. Although all five of us Bennet girls were out in society, it would be a rather scandalous thing should our three youngest sisters be married prior to ourselves.

With simple deduction, I figured the answer to his question. My mother would not likely have shared this gossip with father were the gentleman letting Netherfield Place married.

"Single, yes, my dear Mr. Bennet, and of large fortune. Four, even five thousand a year."

Lydia squealed in excitement, gathering Kitty's hands in her own. The two danced about the room, all ridiculousness and youth.

"How lovely for our girls, do you not think, Mr. Bennet?"

"I am sure I do not know what you mean. What could this gentleman possibly mean to them?"

I stood from my chair, deciding that now may be a good time to go for a walk. I enjoyed father's teasing, but could only tolerate it for a short time. Mama's plan was surely to marry one of us to the poor, unsuspecting man and Papa knew this to be her desire. I squeezed my dearest sister, Jane's, hand before taking my leave.

I had no interest in such talk of marriage and fortune. It was intellect and human nature that interested me. As such I had resigned myself to never marrying and dying an old maid. I could not abide by a life of performing the role of an obedient and uninteresting wife.

Of my five sisters, my elder sister, Jane, was the most beautiful. In truth, Jane was more beautiful than any woman in town and she was at least thrice as kind as she was beautiful. My two youngest siblings, Kitty and Lydia were good-humored and handsome enough. Mary, next youngest to me, was stern and shy of nature and quite plain. Myself, I could not compare to Jane and often was. I was second in birth and second in fairness. I did not begrudge her this, I loved her too dearly. I had books and cleverness, as well as a sharp wit that often got me into trouble. Although I had left the conversation about the mysterious Mr. Bingley, I must admit that I was intrigued.

A mysterious and single young man of large fortune moving to the countryside did not occur often. Now if he were to be handsome as well, I would be sure he was hiding something. Not that it mattered how handsome or plain the man was, he would have the mothers of all the young unmarried women throwing their daughters at his feet. I cannot be a judge of them, although I question how so many women can be so careless when it comes to their own hearts. I suppose they are not, but simply care more for their wallets than I. If this Mr. Bingley wasn't hiding anything, then he was sure to be a fool. No reasonable man of money left the city for a town like Meryton, no matter how grand he thought Netherfield Park to be. By my mind, he would not last long here, no, he would surely get bored of the society and move on soon enough.

As I walked about the gardens, I imagined what sort of sordid past the man was running from. He was likely to be a perfectly fine gentleman with no scandals in his past. However, I preferred my version of the man. I believed him to be rather nefarious, with a penchant for gambling, opium dens, and brothels. A man of large means and many vices. Perhaps he fell into debt with a dangerous man, and as such, had to flee to the countryside for a life of boredom and relative anonymity. I often delighted in imagining such things. It was improper, and a woman of my standing should pretend to not know of things such as brothels and gambling and opium dens. It was in my nature to ignore such societal pressures, if only in my own mind. Never would I speak such things aloud; I would certainly be sealed in my fate as an old maid if I did. If he were to be a dull, handsome, kindly man, I hoped he would take a liking to my dear Jane. If there were any woman in this world who deserved happiness and a large fortune, it would be Jane.

Lost in my thoughts for quite some time, I did not realize how late it had gotten until my stomach began to ache in hunger. I had walked very near the mile to Meryton, and turned back towards home in order to keep my hunger at bay. Meryton was a small market town a mile from Longbourn, where myself and my family resided. Though small, Meryton was of enough importance to have had a mayor at one point in time. Sir William Lucas, the father of my dearest friend, Miss Charlotte Lucas, held the position. I found myself wishing that the direction of my walk had been towards Lucas Lodge, where they resided. Charlotte was a sensible and intelligent woman of near twenty-seven. She would surely be my companion in life, the two of us old maids together. Alas, I had meandered in the opposite direction and must turn back home, where I was sure to hear more of the mysterious Mr. Bingley and the certainty of which Mama spoke of his plan to marry one of the Bennet sisters.

Surely enough, when I arrived back home, the only conversation to be had was about Mr. Bingley. Papa had continued in his way to refuse meeting and becoming acquainted with the man. His teasing of poor Mama had gotten her nerves in a state. Mrs. Bennet's entire business of life was to get her daughters married to the best sort of man, as it also seemed to be the business of every other mother. If Papa should not call on Mr. Bingley then we should have to rely on the likes of Mrs. Long to acquaint us with the gentleman at the assemblies in town. Jane told me that Papa had teased that Mr. Bingley should prefer Mama out of all the Bennet's, and as such, he shan't call upon him. He did, however, offer that when twenty men of five thousand a year come to town, he should call upon all of them. Though Mama's nerves were suffering, Kitty and Lydia were in the throes of excited and youthful imaginings of the fancy balls and parties they would be invited to once Mr. Bingley arrived, and should he marry either of them, the fancy parties they would have. It was nonsense, for if Mr. Bingley were to choose either of those silly girls over our beautiful Jane, I dare say that Papa would not consent. He would be too skeptical of the man's intentions and quite frankly, his intelligence, to allow him to marry even the silliest of my sisters.

"It is a wonderful excitement, though, do you not think, Lizzy?" Jane asked over the clamour of Kitty and Lydia. She knew my nature to be cynical of newcomers, though I am sure she would be horrified of my imaginings of the revered Mr. Bingley.

"I should very much like it if he were to throw a ball. Private balls are so much nicer than public."

"Oh, I so hope he does have a ball, it's such a nice manner of meeting people," Lydia fretted. "It's so dull here. It would offer great escape and much excitement in our lives," she said with drama.

"How is a dance a nice manner of meeting people?" Mary questioned. "Do you not think conversation is a much better manner in meeting people, in order to discover their true nature and character?"

I responded before my youngest siblings could so to save Mary from their ridicule. "It would seem so. However, it would be much less entertaining."

"I do not care for balls. I think them to be tiresome events, where nothing can be gained but making a fool of oneself dancing."

Lydia and Kitty giggled at their unfortunate sibling.

"I would be delighted if he were to have one. I think it would be great fun," Lydia said, giggling again with Kitty by her side.

"If your father refuses to call upon him, it will not matter if Mr. Bingley throws a thousand balls, for we will not be invited to even one of them," Mrs. Bennet fretted.

Although Mr. Bennet seemed to have refused to call upon the gentleman, I was certain he would become acquainted with him. He was sure to be playing a trick on poor Mama's nerves. Though he tried to appear uninterested in the marriage of his daughters, and certainly uninterested in the advantageous marriages of his daughters, he would be a fool not to care. If Papa were to die, it would leave Mama and my sisters and I at the mercy of one Mr. Collins.

Papa had no sons. Therefore, no matter how unfair it was, his property went to the next male heir, which was our cousin, Mr. Collins. Should we not secure marriages, and advantageous ones at that, our fate would be in Mr. Collins' hands. He could turn us out at any moment should he desire to do so. It would be in our best interest to marry well, as such was our position.

Should Papa want to secure our futures, he would have to advocate for the lot of us by calling upon Mr. Bingley. It would be a shame if we were to be required by circumstance to rely on Mrs. Long or the likes of which to make us acquainted with the gentleman. Mama was sure that she would not introduce us, as she had two unmarried nieces of her own.

In the end, Papa was among the first to call upon Mr. Bingley. Near a fortnight after the news that Mr. Bingley had procured Netherfield Park did he arrive. Papa refused to lend any information about the gentleman—whether he seemed good natured, was handsome, or the like. It was a dreadful tease of him to do so, but the news of his calling upon Mr. Bingley sent the house into uproar. As was custom, Mr. Bingley ought to return the call and come here to Longbourn. That begged the question of when he would arrive and how long he would stay for. Mama went into a nervous tizzy about what should be served for dinner should he stay and Lydia and Kitty were excitedly giggling and wondering if he should like their hats.

Mr. Bingley returned Papa's call only a couple days after Papa's visit. It was terrible timing, as my sisters and I, as well as Mama, were not present for his visit. He was clearly a man of good manners, or at the very least, feigned his manners well. Mama sent an invitation to Netherfield for Mr. Bingley to dine with us, but Mr. Bingley was forced to decline, as he was heading back to London. Mama's nerves went into a panic at this news. She could never marry her daughters to the gentleman should he not stay long enough for her to even attempt to pawn one of us off on him.

It was not until we visited Mrs. Lucas that we learned any details about the gentleman. As such was Papa's nature, he had little reason for shielding Mr. Bingley's nature from us. Mrs. Lucas informed us that he was a kind-natured man who was fond of dances and balls and, by all accounts, handsome. It seemed to be far too fortunate for all of us single women that such a man should move here, solidifying in my mind the man's sordid past.

She also gave us reason as to why Mr. Bingley had returned to London. As Mr. Bingley was so fond of balls, he had gone back to London to bring a large party back to accompany him at the public ball in a fortnight. Mama delighted in this news.

Chapter Two:
The Public Ball

It was at the public ball where we were finally acquainted with Mr. Bingley. He and his party arrived fashionably late. His guests were as much the talk of the party as he was. Gossip about his guests had run rampant throughout town while he traveled all the way to London to gather them. Such a trip was worthy of gossip no matter who the traveler. The fact that this traveler in particular was of such wealth made the gossip all the more scandalous.

It was rumored that his party was to be near a dozen. Lydia speculated that Mr. Bingley was sure to bring all the most beautiful women in London with him. She spent days sulking, certain that none of them would ever be married to him, as he was sure to be in love with one of these imagined women that he spent time with in London. Kitty believed that his party would be full of the most fashionable women that she'd ever lay eyes on, and hoped that there would be plenty of handsome men in the party, as well.

The fashionably late arrival of Mr. Bingley and his party meant that every eye at the ball was on them. True, this would have been the case regardless, but their arrival nearly stopped the entire ball.

The music was momentarily interrupted when they stepped into the meeting hall, which put a pause on the dancing, as well.

He walked in with the grandeur and attitude that should be expected from a man earned five thousand a year. The party was but four and Mr. Bingley. Two ladies and two men. The women were soon known to be his sisters, Mrs. Hurst and Miss Bingley, and one of the men his brother-in-law, Mr. Hurst.

Upon the discovery that the two women were of relation to Mr. Bingley, interest in them considerably lessened. Prior to this discovery, the opinions of the female guests of Mr. Bingley were almost spiteful in nature, but as soon as the fear of competition was proved to be false, the opinions of his sisters changed drastically.

In truth, the women appeared to be snobbish. They stood with their arms crossed and their noses upturned. It was slight, and without proper observation, I don't believe that any other would have noticed their attitudes. To me, it was clear that they were none too happy to be at the public ball, or even in Meryton at all. Should Mr. Bingley grow to love any woman in town, I suspected that at least one of his sisters would disapprove of the match.

There was nothing remarkable about the brother-in-law. He appeared to be a gentleman, maybe not very discerning or intelligent, but kind enough. He was certainly oblivious to his wife's disregard of the people of Meryton.

Mr. Bingley himself was quite handsome, and good-natured as they come. Although initially suspicious of such a man, as I met him, he convinced me he could never be the type to frequent any kind of dubious establishment or commit any such nefarious act as I imagined him capable.

The same could not be said of his other male companion, who quickly became the subject of everyone's speculation. He was clearly a strange fellow, either much poorer than his compatriots or so wealthy that his state of dress was not of concern to him. The man was handsome, but odd in more than just a singular way. He created more gossip than anyone who ever came through Meryton before him. He was in a state of disarray, completely underdressed for the occasion. His appearance was disheveled, though it did not detract from his handsome features. He was not a pleasant man, of that I was sure, too wrapped up in his own head to care for a moment about social niceties and propriety. Still, I was intrigued by him. Never had I come across such a person.

Although their entrance interrupted the merriment of the night, the interruption only lasted a few moments before all attending were once again dancing and engaging in gossip, no doubt about the new arrivals.

The new arrivals to the ball began conversing with the only people that Mr. Bingley knew well, the Lucases. It was when they were conversing with our dear friends that I first met Mr. Holmes.

Mr. Bingley easily got himself acquainted with all the important people in the room. He was kind and unreserved in manner, and enjoyed every dance there was to be had, with seemingly boundless energy. I'd wager that near half the woman who spoke with Mr. Bingley left the ball smitten with the amiable man, including the married and older women who had the pleasure of making conversation with him. He danced with Jane twice, which pleased Mama more than she could express, though she tried.

In stark contrast, Mr. Holmes danced only twice, once with Mrs. Hurst and then with Miss Bingley, though there were many women in want of a partner. In truth he appeared uncomfortable to be there, as though he felt he was better than the company, since the only woman who he deigned to dance with were within his party. It was my opinion that this was not the case, only that he did not possess the same amiable qualities as his friend, making it harder to easily converse with so many that the man was not familiar with. However, I had no cordial feelings towards him or pity for his predisposition to be unfriendly.

His behavior did not go unnoticed by the other women at the ball, and he was quick to lose favor with Mama as he insulted me directly. I sat out but two dances because of the shortness of men at the ball, and I sat near enough to Mr. Holmes and Mr. Bingley to overhear their conversation. The two men were discussing the dance, and specifically the women in attendance.

"I have never seen such incredibly beautiful women in my entire life!" Mr. Bingley exclaimed. His breath came fast. He had barely taken a moment from dancing. "You should engage in another dance, Holmes, instead of brooding by yourself."

"I have no such intention to dance," Mr. Holmes replied, taking no true offense at his friend's jibe. "I must disagree with you on your first account, though. You were engaged in dance with the only handsome woman in the room."

I felt my heart leap as the man eyed my dearest Jane and I heard Mr. Bingley agree with the statement enthusiastically. I hoped in my heart of hearts that his finding her beautiful would grow into something more. I had not seen my Jane so happy in some time as when she was dancing with Mr. Bingley. What little I knew of him, his nature seemed as though it would complement Jane's. Although Mr. Holmes said that Jane was the only handsome woman there, with I'm sure the exception of Mr. Bingley's own sisters, this was not the offending remark.

"You are too harsh, Holmes. One of her sisters is behind you now. She is quite handsome and I dare say agreeable."

I found myself flattered by the comment. I was unused to such claims. It was not often that one heard such compliments so freely given. A compliment given face-to-face was not something that could be trusted, but a compliment given when the complimenter did not know the one they were complimenting could hear must by default be the truth. I would gladly take *quite handsome* and possibly *agreeable*, especially when being compared with Jane.

"She has an interesting intelligent look about her, I'll give you that. But I am not in such a desperate rush to find a wife." He then went on to urge his friend to go back to Jane before another man gained her affection.

I shared the story eagerly and with a laugh to my friends. I delighted in all things ridiculous. Though I retold the story with a smile, it would be a lie to say I was not hurt by the comment. Charlotte Lucas knew that my smile concealed my hurt, and tried to offer me comfort, but I did not welcome her kindness, as it made me feel uneasy to speak about my feelings. I was surprised that someone could so quickly sum up my personality in a mere glance. Was I that transparent?

No one appeared to know much about Mr. Holmes - there was a deeper sense of mystery surrounding the man. No one could be sure if he came from money or not, though it was assumed he did based simply on the company he kept. With the way Mr. Bingley's sisters turned their noses up at us common folk, no one believed that either of them would sully their reputations by lowering themselves to not only associate themselves with someone of low standing, but to travel with them as well.

No one seemed to know who he was, or for that matter, anything else about him at all.

It was not much later that some of his mystery was lifted. The man was not mysterious because he didn't want to share about himself. Quite the opposite, when asked a question, he responded honestly and without hesitation. His inability to engage in conversation was what shrouded him in mystery, his quiet and discerning demeanor. When someone queried where the man lived, he responded that he lived at 221 B Baker Street. This caused a flurry of reaction among the ball's guests. It was rather unusual for a man of means to live in an apartment.

"Did you hear that the strange man Mr. Bingley brought with him, Mr. Holmes, is a detective of some kind?" Charlotte informed me.

"I do not much care to hear about Mr. Holmes, clearly I am too intelligent for him, my dear Charlotte." I said dramatically, teasing my friend.

She laughed at my quip, but her expression was one of slight pity. I loved her, but begrudged her for knowing me so well. She knew all my secrets, even the ones I did not know I held. It was she who understood me better than any other, even better than Jane. Jane did not share my cynicism, and thusly could never fully know me. I did not share her optimism, so I could never truly know her. This did not change how fond we were of one another. Charlotte and I had much differing opinions, but we shared the same general outlook on life.

"Well, he's quite right. No man will look at you if your nose is always stuck in a book. I find it fascinating, and quite gruesome. Mr. Holmes solves crimes in London. He lives in an *apartment*!" Lydia said, interrupting mine and Charlotte's conversation. She and Kitty had enjoyed the company of many men and the pair of them had spent near the entire night dancing. Although they were ridiculous and silly girls, they were good-humored and their nature was such that men took interest in them. I oft worried about the two of them, Lydia more than Kitty. Both of them were too consumed by the idea of men, making us all appear as ridiculous as them. Kitty simply followed in Lydia's footsteps, mimicking her elder sister's actions. Should Lydia ever do something foolish, Kitty would likely follow.

"Do you think that Mr. Holmes has ever studied a murder case?" Lydia asked, scandalized at the thought of it.

Unfortunately for her, Mama overheard this question.

"Lydia! Mind your tongue. How could you discuss such things? And in *public*?" Mama admonished Lydia.

Should this question have been asked in private, in the comfort of our home, Mama should not have cared such or have been so upset by the question. That Lydia asked in public was her true offense. Mama cared for our public reputation, though she often forgot herself when she obliged herself too much in libations.

"Mr. Bingley mentioned that Mr. Holmes has worked a multitude of cases, but the details of which were certainly not appropriate to discuss in public," Jane said, coming upon our conversation. She was quick to end the conversation before any of my siblings were able to bring ridicule to the family. Jane was never improper. Her demeanor simply did not allow for such diversion from societal niceties.

"I am absolutely uninterested in whatever cases the man has worked. He does not dress like a gentleman or participate like Mr. Bingley. He is arrogant in nature," Mama said.

It was then that Mr. Bingley came to beg Jane for another dance, though he only need ask. Dear Mama near jumped out of her skin when he arrived, not expecting him to join the conversation at such an unfortunate point in her speech. Whether Mr. Bingley heard her hateful words or not, he gave no indication. The mischievous part of my soul hoped that he had, so that he may extend our feelings of distaste to Mr. Holmes. The politer part of myself hoped he had not heard, so to not offend Mr. Bingley himself. I should not want our shameful comments to negatively impact Jane's prospects.

"Miss Bennet, would you do me the distinct honor of joining me in this next dance?" he asked Jane.

Mr. Bingley made his request with a jovial smile. He had a strong confidence in societal conversations, something his friend lacked. Either Mr. Bingley did not have the intelligence to be concerned with the finer points of conversation nor the opinions that were formed about the man during conversation or he was simply wealthy enough that he didn't have to be concerned with such matters. Mama went from startled by Mr. Bingley's presence to incredibly pleased by it. I think Mama was even happier than Jane, her marital scheme taking such great shape so early into their meeting.

"Nothing would please me more than to take this next dance with you," Jane agreed, taking Mr. Bingley's arm as they moved to the dance floor.

Mama's face beamed with personal satisfaction as she watched them begin the dance. The woman would surely take credit for the sun rising should she be able to. Her face twisted into a scowl as she noticed the disheveled figure of Mr. Holmes to have been standing near to Mr. Bingley before he exited to the dance floor, leaving him near to us. He was scowling, as well, a face that could be compared to a thunderstorm.

"Mr. Holmes, why do you not dance? There are far more women here and the men are scarce," Mama prodded him, trying to goad the man into admitting that he was of the mind that he was better than the rest attending the ball.

"I do not partake in dancing often," was his response, and he spoke emphasizing every word he said. "It is a silly distraction which I cannot abide by, ma'am."

"Should you not engage in such silly distraction, as you call it, as you are in attendance at a ball?

Without dance, one cannot much call it a ball, especially when so many young ladies are being dismissed so easily by the lack of men in attendance," I said with a mischievous grin.

To anyone hearing our conversation, it would sound like a simple observation of the lack of men at the dance. Mr. Holmes did not react in a chagrined or defensive manner as I expected of him.

"It is not the politest thing of me, no, but for me, dancing is not the enjoyable part of a ball."

Mama had become engaged in conversation with Miss Lucas, and Lydia had been swept onto the dance floor once again. It was really just myself and Mr. Holmes present for our discussion. He was handsome, yes, but I found him to be of very peculiar character. I was more intrigued by this odd man than I wanted to admit to myself.

"Pray, tell me, should you not enjoy dancing at a ball, what part *do* you find enjoyable?"

It surely was not the drink, as the man had not had a sip of any libations since he had arrived. I myself doubted that he had much enjoyment in conversing as he had not engaged many outside of his own party in much discourse. Aside from discussion, drink, and dance, I was curious to know what Mr. Holmes found enjoyable about a ball, as to my eye, those were the instrumental pieces to make a ball.

"Observation," he responded. "Miss Bennet, observation is my true joy in life."

"What have you observed this evening, then?"

"Lots," he said, a grin spreading across his face. "The young gentleman over there," as he nodded his head to the opposite side of the room where a young man stood, "has relieved the purses off of three unsuspecting people already, and that woman over there is almost certainly engaged in an affair with more than one of the young men in this room, all of whom are jealous of one another. Likely they will engage in a brawl of some sort later this very eve to win the fair maiden's heart."

I studied the man and the woman that Mr. Holmes indicated in his observations. I could not see anything indicating them as dubious at first. Only upon further investigation did I notice that the man Mr. Holmes indicated as a pickpocket had a rather large bulge on his lower back where he had stuffed the purses. The woman, though I never would have come to the conclusion on my own, certainly had affairs with the men she danced with, cycling through them. She was too informal with them, more comfortable and far too close with the men she was entertaining. It was incredible to see.

"How could you tell all of that from just from observing?"

"The same way that you were able to see it once I showed you the clues which you were seeing but not understanding."

I continued to look about the room. I was curious to see just how Mr. Holmes could predict that the gentlemen competing for the lady's affection would duel later in the evening. I supposed it would just be an educated guess, that the men she was pitting against one another were showing signs of tension and agitation.

"Is this how you solve crimes, Mr. Holmes?"

He was surely an arrogant man, but I supposed that with such intelligence, arrogance was easy to come by, almost a side effect.

"That is exactly how I solve crimes, Miss Bennet."

Chapter Three:
The Man In The Militia

It took time for the excitement of the ball to wear off. Just as Mr. Holmes predicted, a fight broke out not long before the ball was supposed to end. It was all the town could talk about, the most exciting thing to have happened in Meryton in a long time. Combined with the excitement surrounding Mr. Bingley and his party, gossip ran rampant through the town.

Mama was at her best; gossip and matchmaking were her two callings in life. Her talents in them were unmatched by any other.

Mr. Bingley should have been the talk of the town, but he was outshone by the poor young woman's scandal. The fight was so scandalous that the young woman in question went to stay with her aunt and uncle in London. It was customary for these young ladies caught up in scandals to take some time away until society forgot. Society never really forgot, though. It might move on to another scandal, but there was no forgetting any of them. I pitied her, and her family more, for they were made to appear ridiculous and that stain should never leave them. There was no mercy when a woman besmirched her good name.

The men involved with the woman were not granted the same treatment. The gentlemen were given the freedom to go about their lives as though nothing had happened.

Mama had spent most of her time discussing how Jane and Mr. Bingley danced together twice. Mr. Bingley had not danced with any other women more than once. She was certain that these two dances meant the two should be a love match for certain. I knew both were smitten with one another, for it was not hard to tell. Jane had been all smiles since the two met, and although she was usually of this disposition, I could see that she was happier than was typical. I should hope for her a happy marriage to the gentleman Mr. Bingley, should they begin to know each other better. It was an advantageous marriage to be sure, but I dreamt that she should have a happy marriage with the man, not just with his money.

Once the excitement of the ball died down, there was new excitement to be had. The militia was coming through Meryton. Lydia and Kitty were beside themselves with glee at the thought of meeting an officer.

It came at a poor time, though, as our cousin Mr. Collins had come to join us for an undetermined amount of time. The purpose of his visit was not lost to me, as he was an unmarried man and effectively all our belongings were his. The man was here to take his pick of a wife. Should he attempt to choose Jane, Mama would surely intervene on behalf of her.

She was convinced that Mr. Bingley should be making an offer of marriage to her shortly. I felt this to be hasty, but after being acquainted with Mr. Collins, I did not believe that he would be a good match for any woman, but especially not for Jane. Should Mama redirect his attentions, I worried onto whom they should turn.

Mr. Collins had dedicated himself to the church as a clergyman. He did seem more concerned with his patron, Lady Catherine, than with God, though. He was a silly man, narrow-minded and pompous. He subjected us all to speeches about God and the ways of mankind that seemed never to end. Papa was at the end of his wits listening to Mr. Collins' long-winded sermons.

The man was, according to himself, attempting to extend an olive branch to Papa. His father and my father had long ago had a disagreement that resulted in the pair of them no longer speaking. I had no inkling of the details of their disagreement, but it must have been great. There was much tension between Mr. Collins and Papa because he was the son of the man with whom Papa disagreed and he was set to inherit all our belongings. That tension was not made better by Mr. Collins' insufferable nature.

It was a nice reprieve for Papa that we had Mr. Collins join us to Meryton. It was undoubtably no reprieve for us, though. Mr. Collins was uncomfortable with going into town with us; it was silly frivolity in his eyes, and with Lydia and Kitty falling over the officers and giggling, he was most shocked by their behavior. Aside from officers, only new ribbons or hats could keep their attention. Mr. Collins' sermon was cut short by their obvious disinterest as they went from shop to shop, their attention being taken by near every new excitement in town. Mary had declined to come along, seeing no enjoyment in going to town, and as such, Papa and Mary got a much needed break from our unwelcome company.

Mr. Collins ceased his incessant speech when we came upon two handsome gentlemen that drew Lydia and Kitty's attention as soon as their eyes fell upon them. I cannot say that how handsome the gentlemen were was lost on me. Upon some conversation, we became acquainted with Mr. Denny and Mr. Wickham. They were indeed handsome, and quick in conversation. Lydia was particularly drawn to Mr. Wickham, though he seemed not to be interested in her. He directed many a question at me, though. The attention flattered me and I enjoyed our teasing discussion. I did enjoy speaking with them, but my curiosity was not particularly piqued until we met Mr. Holmes and Mr. Bingley while we were walking along the country road heading back towards our homestead. The two were on horseback, on a ride into town.

Most everything about the interaction seemed exceedingly normal, except for Mr. Holmes' and Mr. Wickham's reactions to one another. Their interaction was full of subtle intricacies. The way they posed their bodies gave the impression as though they were once acquainted with one another. Mr. Wickham's jaw tightened as the two men on horseback greeted us and the two only offered each other a terse nod in acknowledgement.

"Miss Bennet, how wonderful it is to see you again!" Mr. Bingley exclaimed. He forgot himself in only addressing Jane and quickly corrected this obvious and telling oversight. "And, of course, all the other Miss Bennets. Wonderful to see you all," he stammered.

Lydia and Kitty held back their raucous laughter, but not very well. They found humor in Mr. Bingley's eagerness to see Jane. I found some humor in his inability to hide it, but more than that, my heart soared as the two of them locked eyes and instantly lit up.

I hoped that maybe Mr. Collins would observe their interactions and not make an offer of marriage to Jane, but I did not trust his capability to understand the finer points of conversation and thusly did not believe that he would take any notice. When I turned to observe him, I found him paying no attention to the conversation at hand as he stood uncomfortably far behind the rest of the group.

"When shall you throw your ball, good sir?" Lydia quizzed Mr. Bingley before Jane could respond. She waved the ribbons that she had gotten in town about the air. "You see, I have purchased ribbons for it already, and you have promised to throw one! When shall it be?"

"Beautiful ribbons, Miss Bennet. Just smashing. The ball shall take place in haste so you do not waste your lovely ribbons," he responded with a large smile.

Mr. Holmes shifted uncomfortably on his horse, ready to leave post haste. I could see the discomfort in his body, how he poised himself on his horse. He was rigid and doing everything he could not to look back in Mr. Wickham's direction. With a curt nod towards myself, Mr. Holmes reared his horse and galloped away. Mr. Bingley startled at his friend's sudden departure.

"I do apologize, madams, sirs. We are on a tight schedule and must be off presently!"

Mr. Bingley was all manners and politeness, just as Jane was. Not only did they share a proclivity for manner, they also shared an authenticity to their politeness that was rare in civilized society. Most everyone shielded their true selves in their manners. They never meant the words that society required them to say. Jane and Mr. Bingley were a different sort. They meant all that they said. I viewed Jane's expression as she watched him ride off. Her subtlety hid her emotions well, as she rarely shared her true emotions, even shielding her true feelings from me, but I could see how honest the joy and affection she felt for Mr. Bingley was.

Mr. Wickham relaxed the moment Mr. Holmes left. The effect of his departure was instantaneous and palpable. Before their departure, the air had a near tangible feeling of tension, though none of my companions seemed to have noted the change.

As we continued on, our larger group divided into natural smaller ones. Lydia and Kitty ran jovially ahead of the group, discussing their ribbons and the excitement of the ball that Mr. Bingley had promised to throw. He had been so disappointed by how early the public ball ended that he said he would throw his own at Netherfield Park. Jane was engaged in conversation with Mr. Denny. I walked beside Mr. Wickham, grateful for the opportunity to ask him about the tension between himself and Mr. Holmes.

"Are you well acquainted with Mr. Holmes, sir?" I inquired.

Mr. Wickham looked at me quizzically, but as he saw my face, he must have realized how sure I was in my conviction that they had known each other at one point. I knew from their interaction that they had a past with one another and it was not a pleasant one.

"No, I never knew the man very well. He was hired on as a detective for a case that, frankly, ruined my life," he responded with more honesty than I had expected, especially as the details of his past with Mr. Holmes were certainly sordid and personal.

"I am sorry to hear that."

"And you, do you know him well?"

I shook my head in dissent. I felt slight guilt that I had brought up what was clearly a sore subject for the man. I did not know either man very well, as

I had just met them both briefly and only quite recently.

"No, I met him briefly when I became acquainted with Mr. Bingley. I have not become well acquainted with him at all."

"Well, if I were you, I would consider myself lucky to not be acquainted with a man such as Mr. Holmes." Mr. Wickham was vehement in his disenchantment with the man.

"If you don't mind my prying, may I ask what the nature of your disagreement with the man is?" I carried the conversation on, surprised by the candid nature of Mr. Wickham's words. I found it difficult to tell if he spoke with such candor with just anyone, or if there was a significant ease to conversing with one another specifically.

"I grew up with no real father of my own. My true father was a man who took me under his wing and taught me to be a good man. He had another son, though, who was jealous of me. It only got worse after the man died and left a sizeable portion of his estate to me. I was slated to join the church, but his son took all that away from me. He accused me of something that I simply did not do and Mr. Holmes was the man he hired to, as they called it, prove I did so." He spoke matter-of-factly, as though he had accepted the sad truth that he was unable to do anything to change his past or prove that he had not done whatever was accused.

"I'm sorry that happened to you. It sounds like an awful ordeal." This was not sufficient in apologies for what horrible things poor Mr. Wickham had gone through, but I had no other words of comfort to offer the man.

"It happened a long time ago. I cannot help but be bitter about it, but I have done my best to move on from the injustice."

He certainly had bitterness left in him, as made evident by his hateful speech against Mr. Holmes. It was my feeling that Mr. Holmes had made many an enemy. Despite his dismissal of me at the ball I had warmed up to the gentleman as we discussed the complexities of observing human behavior. Focally I sympathized with Mr. Wickham and felt certain that whatever accusation made against him was sure to be false, however I did not believe that Mr. Holmes would wilfully give false evidence. It did not seem to be in his nature to deceive in such a manner.

I did not press Mr. Wickham further on the matter, as he was clearly not willing to give more detail than he already had. It was sure to be a minor infraction, as the man was not imprisoned in any capacity. Still, however minor the infraction, the repercussions were grand, clear as day. Mr. Wickham had lost all of his inheritance and could no longer pursue the life of the church.

It was not much farther that we were forced to part ways with the officers.

"It was a pleasure meeting you fine young ladies," Mr. Denny said, offering a small bow of the head in departure. "Unfortunately, this is where we must leave you, but we shall leave you in the capable hands of Mr. Collins."

He nodded towards Mr. Collins, who had stirred up enough courage to join Mr. Denny and Jane in their conversation. Mr. Collins responded with an over pronounced bow, sweeping his right foot forward in dramatic fashion.

"Shall we see you at the ball at Netherfield Park?" Lydia asked.

"I would not miss it," Mr. Denny responded.

He started to turn away, before stopping to wait for Mr. Wickham.

"Shall you go to the ball, too?" I asked, rather hopeful.

"Should you wish it, then I shall be there, Miss Bennet."

His reply made my cheeks flush. I was unused to attention such as that from men, though I did not mind it. He bowed politely and left with Mr. Denny.

I believe that must have been the last time I saw Mr. Wickham alive.

Our party made our way back to our home in Longbourn. Mr. Collins seemed to relax when the two officers departed. He did not enjoy their company. As far as I could see, he did not much enjoy the company of anyone but the sound of his own voice and possibly his patronage the Lady Catherine De Bourgh. He seemed to be a sham of a man, a conglomeration of quotes and sayings that were not used in real life, but were lines one could read from a page. All of his conversation was directly quoted from literature, and obviously practiced a multitude of times. There was nothing genuine about the man.

After a gruelling dinner and evening reading from Mr. Collins, Jane and I were thankful to leave for our room, where we could enjoy a reprieve from Mr. Collins' incessant chatter. The pair of us enjoyed our evenings together. Our room was where we shared the most intimate details of our souls, where we could be the most ourselves.

"Mr. Bingley is just what a gentleman should be," Jane said, a smile stretched across her face. "I am so pleased to have met him."

This kind of statement was as good as saying she loved him. Jane was so private with her feelings, I often found her to be a mystery, sure that she had more to say than she ever allowed herself to. I, on the other hand, could never hold my tongue, allowing my thoughts and emotions to run freely into the world. I did not have the talent that Jane possessed in hiding my emotions. By nature, I was less tactful than she.

"I am pleased for you, my dear, sweet Jane." I was overwhelmed by affection for my sister. "What are your thoughts on Mr. Wickham?" I asked.

I had continued to think about him long after we parted ways. I did not know how to think about the man, but I could not stop myself from thinking of him. He was handsome to be sure, one of the most handsome men I had ever laid eyes on, but I did not trust him. He seemed too charming to me, as though he had a secret that he had kept for a long time. It had to have something to do with what he had been accused of doing and that Mr. Holmes proved to be true.

"He seems like a perfectly agreeable man. Very handsome," she replied, teasing me.

I found him attractive, but there was more to him than met the eye. My thoughts were consumed by him and Mr. Holmes. I wanted desperately to know their history. Clearly, the case was something that Mr. Wickham wanted to hide. I did not blame him, as if I were accused of a crime, I am sure that I would want that information to remain private, but my very nature was to be curious about such things.

"Yes, he is. Very."

I could tell that Jane had been exhausted by the day. In truth, I found myself tired by the day's activities, as well. Mr. Collins had read to us for near an hour after dinner. His monotone voice, combined with the long walk to and from town, rendered us all overcome with sleepiness.

"He and Mr. Holmes know one another."

Jane had closed her eyes but had not yet fallen asleep. She did not inquire with words, but instead made a soft hmm sound in interest.

"Apparently Mr. Holmes helped in a false accusation against Mr. Wickham for some kind of crime or scandalous act."

Jane looked at me through one open eye. "That's quite a story. I'm sure that whatever the case, it was a misunderstanding of sort."

I laughed at her, always wanting to think the best of everyone.

"I bet he killed someone," I said to scandalize her.

It worked, as her eyes sprung open in shock. "Lizzy! How could you say such a horrible thing?"

I smiled at her. She gave me an exasperated expression before turning over and blowing out the candle that kept our room alight. This signified that she decided that it was time for the both of us to fall asleep. I could hear her soft snoring after just a moment of silence.

I, however, could not get to sleep so easily. My thoughts would not allow me to get any rest. I found my mind wandering over the events of the prior fortnight. Jane had met her match, so long as Mr. Collins did not extend a hand of marriage to her. I knew that if Mama caught wind of it, she would manipulate it so that it did not happen. She would want one of us to marry him, however. It would ensure the family's safety forever, and myself and my sisters would not have to worry about being turned out of our home after Papa died. Although this would be her desire, she would not have Jane marry him if she could help the situation. The advantageous marriage between Mr. Bingley and Jane was worth protecting, even if it meant that she would hazard offending Mr. Collins. I knew that should she be able to redirect his sights, they would then be set on me. I should not accept any proposal of marriage he would offer. This would be a selfish act on my part, but I could not abide by more than a few hours time with Mr. Collins, not to mention an entire life-time with the man. It was my hope that Mama would offend Mr. Collins, not enough that he might turn us all out on the street, but enough that he would no longer wish to marry any of us or spend much time at Longbourn.

My mind continued to wander back to Mr. Wickham and Mr. Holmes. I knew that their past was important in someway. Both gentlemen had captured my attention for different reasons, but their hold on me was strong. I knew Mr. Wickham had also captured Lydia's attention. She had spent most of our walk in conversation with Mr. Denny, but even more of it staring at Mr. Wickham. There was a part of me that felt Mr. Wickham could not be trusted, and that part manifested itself not when he informed me of his sordid dealings with Mr. Holmes, but in the exchange of glances between he and Lydia.

Chapter Four:
Death At The Ball

"I will do your chores for you for a month, Lizzy, please!" Lydia begged, chasing me around the upper floor of the house. The house had been in an uproar with us all getting ready for the ball at Netherfield Park. Lydia had been asking me to lend her my best shoes for the ball.

"Lydia, you owe me months of chores already," I responded.

Lydia constantly offered up chores as payment for borrowing clothing items and the like. She never repaid them, although Jane and myself usually lent her things regardless. She wanted everything that we had, but that was the way of younger sisters, so we allowed her this one indulgence.

"I promise, Lizzy. Please, I need them for the ball."

"What if I need them for the ball?" Although I had no intention of not allowing Lydia to use my shoes, I could not give them up easily. Then she would be a nightmare. If she knew we gave our clothes up willingly, she would never stop requesting them of us. She batted her eyes at me dramatically. "Alright, fine. One month of chores, though, Lydia."

She jumped for joy and wrapped me in a hug before running off to get my shoes.

"She might do them this time. I believe she may want those shoes enough to actually do chores for them," Jane said, coming up behind me, watching our little sister bound down the hallway.

"I doubt it. Once she has them, she will not put another thought to doing the chores," I replied. Although the words sounded harsh, I did not mean them in such a way. I said them with a smile. I knew my younger sister well and loved her despite her quirks.

I had never seen Lydia and Kitty so excited. They could not wait for the ball. Mr. Bingley had announced it not long after our encounter on the way back from town. His sister had been the one to extend the invitation to us, which greatly upset our Mama. She felt it was a slight against Jane, as Mr. Bingley did not extend the invitation personally. Jane did not feel offended. She was thankful that Caroline, Mr. Bingley's sister, was extending her welcome. It felt as though the invitation coming from her was some kind of precursor to inviting her to join the family. Of course, the way Jane and I felt may have been our own hopes skewing our interpretation of the act.

It had been a long while since there was something so extravagant to look forward to in town. Jane had let her guard down for the first time in a while. She was so happy to see Mr. Bingley. From my perspective, it appeared as though the ball was a lavish excuse for Mr. Bingley and Jane to see one another. Of course, I did not know Mr. Bingley's mind, but it felt like this would be the case on his side of the matter, as well.

The only unenthusiastic member of the Bennet family was, of course, Mary. She had no interest in balls and had come near to refusing to go, though she knew as well as I that attendance at the Bingley ball would be compulsory. My only hope for Mary at the ball was that she would not try to take up the piano and entertain the guests. She had talent playing the piano forte, but had very little talent in singing. She often took up the piano forte in an attempt to entertain. Typically, people were kind and allowed her to play without the humiliation of discovering that her talent was not so great. I feared that the guests at Mr. Bingley's ball would not be so kind. Papa had already urged Mary to avoid the piano forte, his fears being similar to my own.

Even Papa had become excited to go to the ball, and it was a break in his usual character. His comfort was books and his study. He did not much like being sociable, so it surprised me that he seemed as though he could not wait to go to the ball. I thought it might be his excitement for Jane to be with Mr. Bingley, but I could not be sure of his reasons.

When we arrived, we were greeted warmly by our hosts. Netherfield Park was magnificent on its own, but decorated for a ball, it seemed to me to be an unreal sight. The gentlemen and ladies studded the estate with their beauty. I myself could not be swayed by beauty alone, but I could not deny that my breath had been taken away by the sight. Mr. Bingley could hardly stop himself from speaking with Jane longer than would be appropriate as we entered. Caroline, Mr. Bingley's sister, stopped him from paying too close attention to Jane and continued on in the line of welcoming us into their home. She was a shrewd woman, who certainly understood that her brother had budding feelings for Jane. When I saw her usher Jane through, interrupting her brother's prolonged greeting, I began to suspect that she was not as supportive of the match as I had desired her to be.

Mr. Collins continued to bring embarrassment to us. He discovered that Mr. Holmes would be in attendance and had begun his search. In fact, he was in search of any name that had status in attendance. Mr. Collins seemed to be the type to find status in his acquaintances, and searched for more at every chance. The true reason for his desire to meet Mr. Holmes was that he was well acquainted with the nephew of Miss Catherine De Burgh. His appreciation for the woman extended beyond just herself and her family members, to their acquaintances as well. I was engaged in conversation with Mama, Jane, and Caroline when I noticed that Mr. Holmes stood nearby to us, conversing with a group of people, and that Mr. Collins was closing in on the man. I turned my focus away from the conversation at hand and listened in on Mr. Collins' attempt at introducing himself to Mr. Holmes.

"Hello, Mr. Holmes. It is an honor to make your acquaintance," Mr. Collins said with a stiff bow towards Mr. Holmes, who jumped at the intrusion and looked down upon the squirrelly man.

"Yes," he said curtly, returning the bow. "And you are?"

"Mr. Collins, sir."

Mr. Holmes nodded again at the man before turning away. It was then that Mr. Collins coughed to capture his attention once again. Mr. Holmes turned to face him, clearly finding the man as much of an annoyance as I did.

"Sorry, did you need assistance?"

"No, of course not," he stammered. "I know about your work as a consulting detective."

"Do you need detecting?"

"No, you misunderstand me, sir. My patroness is the Lady Catherine De Burgh. You worked on a case for her nephew not long ago. Mr. Darcy was the name."

Mr. Holmes looked at the man as though he had started to speak a foreign language in the middle of their conversation. I had to stifle a laugh as I digested Mr. Holmes' expression.

"Pleasure to make your acquaintance," Mr. Holmes responded, giving the man another bow, quite obviously feigning respect for Mr. Collins before once again turning away from him and returning to his conversation.

Mr. Collins tried once again to catch his attention, but Mr. Holmes simply pretended to ignore the man's coughs. I had no doubt that Mr. Holmes recalled the exact case that Mr. Collins was bringing up. I could make the safe assumption that his memory was extensive and clear. He seemed far too clever to me to be unable to recall any fact he might need to. When Mr. Holmes turned to face his group, the man met my eye shortly. Though he did not smile, I could sense a mischievous glint in his eyes.

It was not long before he made his way over to Mama, Caroline, Jane, and I along with Mr. Bingley. Mama was overjoyed with Mr. Bingley's appearance. She had been waiting with impatience for him to arrive and ask Jane for a dance. She still felt disillusioned with Mr. Holmes, not wanting to forgive him for his poor social manners.

Mr. Bingley invited Jane to join him for the next dance. Should a person be able to die of happiness, I believe that she could have. Caroline gave another brief but clear indicator that she did not approve of the match. It was not in her words, but her expression. I could see a subtle change in her manner as Mr. Bingley requested that Jane join him on the dance floor. Her face fell slightly and I could imagine her manner of disapproval. We were not so well off as they. It would clearly be an advantageous marriage for Jane. Caroline might not believe that Jane's feelings were genuine, or she simply believed us to be of a lower station than would be proper to marry her brother.

"Miss Bennet, would you do me the honor?" Mr. Holmes asked.

I startled at the request. "I'm sorry?" I asked, although I heard and understood his original question.

"Do me the honor of dancing the next dance with me?"

"It would be my pleasure," I responded immediately.

Mama and Caroline looked equally upset by the request and my subsequent acceptance, though I knew their reasons were different. Mama simply did not like Mr. Holmes, but Caroline was more than just acquainted with him and seemed to enjoy his company. I believed that she felt slighted by being overlooked by Mr. Holmes, especially as she was the only single woman he danced with at the previous ball. I did not think that she had feelings for the man, but rather she felt slighted when any man did not express a preference for her.

Mr. Holmes and I joined each other in the next dance. Dances were interesting, as they were the only time that young men and women were allowed to be engaged in conversation without some kind of chaperone. Although conversations could still be overheard, there was a degree of freedom that was not afforded at any other time. It was because of this that Mr. Holmes asked me to join him in a dance. Never did we share romantic feelings or consider the other in such a manner. Though we became less concerned with public appearances as time went on, oftentimes when the case called for it, we would join one another on the dance floor to have discussions without drawing attention to ourselves. This was the first dance of that nature.

"Miss Bennet, I do believe you have been paying more attention as of late."

"If by paying attention you mean observing, then yes, I have, Mr. Holmes."

"Do you think that you are talented at it?"

I had not considered this question and was caught off guard by it. I did not understand how one was to know if they had talent at observation, as it appeared to be all conjecture unless somehow your observations manifested themselves in physical evidence. A personal observation could not be something one had talent for. Although, it was with this skill Mr. Holmes became a detective.

"I do not know if I understand your query."

"Your deductions from observation, are they accurate? Do you have talent?"

"I am not sure if I am yet able to gauge how accurate my assumptions are."

Mr. Holmes let out a laugh. "Very diplomatic answer, Miss Bennet." He paused briefly as the dance moved us away from one another. "But," he continued, "what you are doing is not making assumptions, but making accurate deductions based on what it is you are observing with your eyes. There are not and should be no assumptions made. True talent in deduction is knowing that."

"Then I suppose I have not been observing and deducting for a long enough period of time to say that I have talent at it. All my observations have only led to conjecture for myself."

"And what conjectures have you made thus far?" The man was quizzing me. Seeing if I had talent in what he was an artist in. I did not know how to react or why he had taken such an interest in my observational skills. For that matter, I had no inkling as to why I had even begun to make such astute observations of those around me. His power of suggestion at the public ball had been enough to make me want to try out deduction and observing for myself. Not that I had never practiced observation before. I was by nature an observer of those around me, but never before had I thought about the conclusions that one could draw based on observation alone. Mr. Holmes would not drop his line of questioning, which began to frustrate me.

"You and Mr. Wickham have an interesting past," I said. "You worked on a case that made him lose everything. He has implied that your deduction was untrue, that you feigned evidence to make him appear guilty of what he did not commit."

"Mr. Wickham never fails to convey how ill I treated him, in his own version of events." The mention of the name did not seem to upset him in the same way the mention of his name upset Mr. Wickham.

"What is your opinion?" he asked. The mention of the man had not bothered him, but the accusation of falsifying evidence did. "That I would do such a thing as feign my testimony to make Mr. Wickham appear guilty?"

There was an anger that I had not thought him capable of behind the words. His profession was his dearest possession in life. I had not seen him show the same level of respect to anything else. Although he appeared more put together than he had at the public ball, his appearance was still disheveled at best, which made him stick out in the current company.

"I do no believe you would." I had made up my mind in this matter. That Mr. Wickham had secrets. To be sure, Mr. Holmes had them as well, but Mr. Wickham not only possessed secrets, but lies. From my perspective, it seemed as though Mr. Wickham was guilty of whatever he had been accused of and simply maintained his innocence in a ploy to garner pity. To avoid taking responsibility for his actions, he blamed Mr. Holmes for what he called false testimony. Mr. Holmes relaxed after I stated this belief. "I think your alliance to the truth and your respect for your position, consulting detective, is far too great for you to be swayed to give false evidence."

"If I did not have my good reputation in solving cases and gathering evidence, then I would have nothing."

Something in the way he spoke expressed to me the truth of how little he would have should he lose his position. A wave of pity for the man washed over me momentarily. He most certainly had only a few people in the world to rely upon.

"I believe that to be true," I responded.

The dance came upon its end, but before it came to a halt, Mr. Holmes lent me a warning: "Guard yourself and your sisters against Mr. Wickham. He is charming, but dangerous news for young ladies of good standing. I have seen how young Lydia looks upon the man, and you must warn her against him. The consequences of the contrary would be detrimental to her and to your family."

With that, he left my side, disappearing into the crowd. Strange, his talent to disappear despite his odd appearance. His warning had left a knot in the pit of my stomach. I surveyed the crowd in the dance hall, looking for Lydia and Mr. Wickham. I had forgotten that Mr. Wickham should be in attendance. The nature of Mr. Holmes' warning made my mind run wild with the possibilities of what Mr. Wickham had done in the past to an unsuspecting young lady of good standing. Lydia was sure to be the most unsuspecting lady I had ever come across and her silliness knew no bounds. She was drawn to Mr. Wickham and I had suspicions that he knew how to take advantage of that. Mr. Holmes had disappeared and I could not locate Mr. Wickham or Lydia. I felt in my heart that something was not right.

"Charlotte, have you seen Lydia this evening?" I asked, joining my dear friend at the outskirts of the room. Charlotte was a dear and had been entertaining Mr. Collins for the better part of the evening. She was now standing alone at the edge of the room, attempting to keep her distance from the man to enjoy a break.

"I have not seen her. I am sorry Lizzy. Is something the matter? You appear rather agitated."

I had become rather distraught from not being able to locate either Mr. Wickham or Lydia. I feared that he was manipulating her into doing things she would otherwise not. Lydia was but fifteen years old and susceptible to the suggestion of men. No matter how foolish, should she believe him to be in love with her, she would go with him.

"I have learned some troubling news about Mr. Wickham, the officer I told you about not long ago. I fear that the two are together."

Charlotte immediately took my concern seriously, her hand raising to her mouth. "I shall help you locate them."

We did not need to search for long before we heard the screams. As I raced in the direction they came from, I could feel in my very soul that the screams were being ripped from Lydia's lungs. The entire ball had taken pause at her shouts, the music stopping abruptly as the screams echoed throughout Netherfield Park.

When I arrived on the scene, I was relieved that Lydia appeared to be alright. They were in a room far from the rest of the gathering. It had not been designed to be a part of the ball that evening and as such was dark, the only light coming from the rooms surrounding it. Mr. Holmes had arrived on the scene prior to myself. He was holding Lydia as she shouted and screamed. My view was obscured by the dark, but I could just make out Mr. Wickham lying on the ground. My thoughts raced to put the pieces of the puzzle together.

It was not until Mr. Bingley came up behind me with a candle that I saw the full scene. Mr. Wickham was lying dead on the ground. He did not appear to be bloody; the cause of death was not apparent. However, there was blood on the wall, the letters "RACHE" written in it. The scene was grisly to be sure. I had never seen such a thing in my life.

As soon as Lydia calmed enough to notice me there, she ran into my arms sobbing.

"He's dead, Lizzy. Mr. Wickham is dead." She repeated the statement over and over again with no pause. The event had traumatized her, as it would most. I myself had a morbid curiosity and wanted to uncover the truth behind his mysterious death.

"This is now a murder scene and investigation. No one may come or go," Mr. Holmes said with authority.

Mr. Bingley nodded, his face pale. As more people came to see the cause of the screams, chaos and commotion began to break out. Women fainted and cried out, men became angry and suspicious. They also wanted to leave, stating they clearly had no part in the death and as such they should be allowed to leave of their own free will.

Mr. Bingley was shaken, but managed to convince near everyone to stay until they could get some answers. Immediately, someone went to notify the police, though we were not equipped for such a crime. It would have to be Mr. Holmes who ran the investigation, at least until the proper authorities could arrive.

"Miss Bennet," Mr. Holmes said to gain my attention, which had been focused on Lydia entirely.

"Yes?" I asked, trying to hold Lydia up. She was conscious, but seemed not to have the ability to keep herself standing.

"I will be requiring your assistance with this case," he answered.

And with that statement, in that moment, my life was forever changed.

Chapter Five:
An Indecent Proposal

Mama and Papa were so concerned with Lydia that they took no notice of me joining in the investigation. Mr. Holmes managed to keep everyone from coming into the room where Mr. Wickham lay dead.

"How can you be sure that he was murdered?" I asked, standing a distance from the body.

He motioned to the word written in blood on the wall.

"There is no blood on Mr. Wickham. Maybe the two incidences are not connected?" I had never seen death before, but I had to imagine that it was not common that a man as young and healthy as Mr. Wickham would be killed without a bloody fight.

"I do not believe in coincidences in the most likely of scenarios. In a situation such as this, they must be related, however odd the circumstances."

I turned my attention from the lifeless body on the ground to the bloody word on the wall. I wondered what it could mean. It was nothing like I had seen before. I was familiar with the German word "rache," meaning revenge, and did not have any illusions about the probability that there were many a man and woman that wanted to exact revenge on the man.

"What do you think it means?"

"I think it's a message," he said in an offhand manner.

"What do you mean, a message?" I queried. It felt as though he was disregarding the significance of the letters entirely. "Could it be the killer trying to tell us something? Rache means revenge in German; perhaps that is the motive here."

Mr. Holmes looked at me with a dry expression of boredom. I got the impression that this was the exact conclusion he had come to, as well.

"The idea of leaving behind this message to tell us why he committed a murder is ludicrous, but I am certain the man meant it as a message telling us the true crime was whatever Mr. Wickham did to the gentleman who committed the murder and the real reason behind the murder of our Mr. Wickham."

"And what do you suggest that is?"

"I have no idea." The man was crouched over the body with a magnifying glass that appeared to have been in his coat pocket the entire time. He lifted Mr. Wickham's hand up, examining it, and placed it back to the ground. In truth, Mr. Holmes appeared to be more comfortable dealing with a corpse than he was dealing with living, breathing people. He was at ease in the crime scene, and I had a front row seat to view how he examined and came to conclusions based on those examinations. I could almost compare it to watching da Vinci with a canvas and a brush, watching Mr. Holmes with a corpse and nothing but a few clues. "This man is sure to have been poisoned."

"Have you deduced this because of the lack of blood or bodily injury?"

"Yes. He also has white residue on the tips of his fingers from a pill of some type. It is my belief that this man ingested a pill that caused his demise."

I could not fathom what would make a man as fit and strong as Mr. Wickham seemingly willingly take a pill that caused his death. I assumed it was willingly as there was no sign of a struggle in the room. If the murder had taken place elsewhere and the body moved, his killer would have to be almost inhumanly strong to move such a man from a different location.

"Do you think he took the pill of his own volition?"

"I would think it so. The residue from the pill is on his own fingers as though he took the pill himself. We shall need to make queries in order to discover who has committed this crime." I had assumed as such would be the case. No investigation was complete without interrogations. It seemed that no matter what evidence could be gathered from the body, the way to find the guilty party was through speaking with the people who witnessed it. Mr. Holmes' tone changed as he looked at me. "I will need to speak with Lydia."

"I know we must, but she will need time to calm herself before we can speak to her." I knew that Lydia would be a key witness to the murder. More than likely, she was the last person to see Mr. Wickham alive, and based on how shaken poor Lydia was, she may have even seen his death. I could still hear Lydia wailing in the distance, where most of the guests had returned to the main hall.

Mr. Bingley had decided that he would send some people home. There were far too many people in attendance to keep them for long. He was preoccupied with ensuring that my family was doing alright, as they were all shaken for Lydia.

Mr. Holmes and I had been observing the crime scene for a while now. He was silent for most of it and I simply stood there watching him make his observations. I guess silent was not the right word for it. He spent most of his time muttering to himself. Were I not already acquainted with the man, I surely would think him to have some kind of insanity. To be frank, though I did know him, I remained unconvinced that he did not have any insanity.

"I think you should be the one to question her, Miss Bennet."

"You want me to interview her?" I had never conducted an interview before and did not know that I could or why Mr. Holmes would want me to. I had not put much thought into why Mr. Holmes had me assisting him at all. It was odd for him to request a woman to assist him in the first place, let alone me, a woman with whom he was barely acquainted. I never asked him that question, the why of it all. I did not much care to. I found myself too wrapped up in the excitement of the case and the intrigue of Mr. Holmes.

"You have a connection to her. She will more willingly speak with you than she would with me."

His response made sense. Lydia would certainly be sure to answer any questions I might ask. I did not want to put her through that, though. She was a fragile girl, and I knew that she would not be able to face what she saw for a second time.

"I cannot rightly ask her questions about what she witnessed tonight yet. She will need time to recover, Mr. Holmes."

"No, we can't wait. She needs to be questioned immediately or she will forget the details that she saw."

I did not disagree with his assessment of the situation, but I still could not question my sister in her state in good conscience. "Let us gather all that we can from here and then go to her for questions."

Mr. Holmes nodded in agreement. "I have gathered most of what is possible from the body and the room." This startled me, as I did not even know what to make of the scene we were looking at. Mr. Holmes grinned at me, as though he enjoyed my ineptitude. "Mr. Wickham took poison that killed him, and he took the pill of his own volition, but he was murdered. There is no blood on the body, but there is the writing on the wall in blood. Given that, the blood must belong to the murderer.

"The murderer would have been someone who held a grudge against the man, but given who

Mr. Wickham was in life, he had no shortage of men and women who had a grudge against him. The murderer was a man, six feet tall, though his feet are disproportionate to his height. He was wearing a square-toed shoe and he smoked a cigar."

"How do you know all that?" I was shocked by how detailed his deductions were. These were not simple observations and assumptions. He pulled distinct and (he seemed sure) accurate facts from the things he observed. Mr. Holmes appeared to be having the best time of his life telling me all that he was able to deduce from his looking around the room.

"Nothing more than simple deduction, Miss Bennet. Shall we question your sister now?" He asked the question with more sensitivity than I expected from the man. He showed little compassion normally, but here he was gentle in his delivery. He knew that I would not stand for an abrasive attack on Lydia. Asking her questions forcefully was not something that I would allow to happen. "We will only ask her what she can handle," he reassured.

"I suppose it is time. She must have calmed down enough. I do not hear her cries any longer. If she is resting, can we allow her to sleep?"

He nodded in agreement.

"Thank you." I was appreciative of this allowance. Should she not be related to me I doubted he would allow such niceties.

As we were leaving, the doctor showed up to take away Mr. Wickham's body.

Mr. Holmes stayed with the doctor, ensuring that nothing aside from the body was disturbed in the crime scene. It would be a few days before officials from Scotland Yard could arrive at Netherfield Park.

I discovered my family huddled together in the drawing room. Mr. Bingley had taken them away from the rest of the crowd in order to give Lydia privacy. He tried offering her a room, but she did not want to be away from everyone. Lydia was still weeping, laying on Mama's lap. Her eyes were closed, though, so I could not be sure if she was sleeping or not. Jane came up to me as I entered the room.

"Lizzy, where have you been?" she asked me in a hushed tone.

"Mr. Holmes wanted me to assist him." She gave me a quizzical look, but I continued before she could ask more questions. "I need to speak with Lydia. Is she doing alright?"

Jane was immediately consumed by concern for our younger sister. Kitty had fallen asleep with her arms wrapped around Lydia. I could see now that Lydia had not fallen asleep. Her eyes were open and they were red with tears and exhaustion as one would expect from anyone who had gone through such an ordeal. Papa was pacing around the room and Mary had clearly fallen asleep a while before, as she was asleep in an arm chair.

"I do not think that she will ever be the same again," Jane whispered, looking back at Lydia with pity.

"Do you think that she will be okay with me asking her about what she may have seen?"

Jane shook her head. "Lizzy, you cannot be considering asking her to relive what she has just seen?"

She was horrified by my query and I could not help but feel an overwhelming sense of guilt for having even considered such a thing. Jane had not asked to make me feel guilt, but that was the result. I could not imagine what the horror of seeing Mr. Wickham's death had done to Lydia.

"Mr. Holmes needs to know what she saw or did not see in order to find out who killed Mr. Wickham."

Papa heard me speaking to Jane although we were whispering our words. "Lizzy, that is not going to happen. Lydia is in no condition to speak, let alone answer questions that she does not have answers for." Papa's voice was stern. He was angry with me for the suggestion.

I was angry with him for impeding the investigation. I had made no indication that my queries would be unanswerable. My plan was quite the opposite. I wanted only to ask her questions she would be able to answer. I readied my reply, but before I could speak, Lydia did.

"What do you need to know, Lizzy?" She sniffled, raising herself from Mama's lap. Kitty did not wake, but moved her own head to Mama's lap and made herself comfortable. Mama was surely horrified by the death of Mr. Wickham, but her maternal instincts had kept her nerves at bay. It was surprising to see how well Mama and her nerves were handling all the excitement. She had started to stroke Kitty's hair as soon as Lydia rose from her seat. "If I can help, Lizzy. Ask me what you need to."

"Are you certain?" I asked Lydia.

She nodded at me. She appeared to be weak, as though it was hard for her to even stand, but she did it. I felt another wave of guilt come over me, although this time it was not because I needed to ask her questions, but because I had believed her to be so fragile that she could not handle it.

"Can you just go through your evening with me, Lydia? Tell me what happened."

"I had been asked to dance by a gentleman, I do not remember who, but before the dance began, Mr. Wickham came up to me." She brought her hand to her face, wiping away a tear. "He said that he could not stop thinking of me from the moment we met. He said many things, to woo me, I suppose, but he suggested we speak privately and I agreed. What a fool I am." She let an angry huff out, as though she were mad at herself for what happened. "When we went to the room, he forced himself on me."

She looked at Papa nervously as she said this. He stopped pacing and his hand went to his mouth in shock and upset, but he said nothing, allowing Lydia to finish her tale. "I ran away to the adjoining room. I was so fearful. He did not follow me, though. I stayed in the other room just shy of an hour, trying to remain hidden. It was then that I heard the thump of him falling. I ran to the room to find him lying there on the ground." It was here in her story that she began sobbing. "I'm sorry," she whispered. She continued to repeat the phrase through her tears as she ran back over to Mama, who opened her arms to her.

My heart broke for Lydia. She had always had an innocence to her that she would never have again. Mr. Wickham had taken that from her even before he had died and before she had seen his lifeless body. A young woman should not have to apologize for a man taking advantage of her. She had been sobbing not just because she had stumbled upon Mr. Wickham's body, but also because of the shame she felt for leaving with him in the first place.

"Thank you, Lydia. You've helped tremendously," I said, kneeling in front of Lydia and stroking her hair. "Thank you."

"He scared me and was a scoundrel to be sure, but that doesn't mean he should be dead," she cried and turned her face into Mama.

Mr. Bingley arrived with an offer for us to stay the night as I made my exit. In the meantime, all the other guests had taken their leave. Once the physician was able to take away Mr. Wickham's corpse, Mr. Holmes had told Mr. Bingley to allow everyone in attendance to leave. He seemed certain that he would be able to find the killer whether the restless group stayed at Netherfield Park or not.

It was not until later that I discovered the real reason Mr. Holmes had allowed all the attendants of the ball to take their leave. He knew that none of them had committed the murder, that the responsible party would be staying—that it must be someone from my own party or Mr. Bingley's.

Chapter Six:
A Small Clue

The next morning, we awoke at Netherfield Park. The lot of us had slept late, as no one wanted to wake and deal with the weight of Mr. Wickham's death. Mr. Bingley was already speaking of leaving Netherfield Park, as he could not bear to stay in a house where such a ghastly thing occurred. Were it anyone else, this kind of speech would render me weary and suspicious, but I knew that Mr. Bingley simply did not have it in his character to commit such a terrible crime.

Mr. Collins had fled back to his homestead as soon as the body had been discovered. He did not want to be a part of something so amoral. I am sure that he would prefer that word of his association with such a heinous act not get back to his patroness. I hoped any dream or wish of marrying either me or one of my sisters had been expunged from his mind with his departure.

Currently, however, I had more pressing matters occupying my thoughts. I had been reeling over Mr. Holmes' description of the assailant. Six feet tall. Small feet. Square-toed shoes. Cigar smoker.

I could not place a man of that description at the ball the previous evening. I continued to go over each man I laid eyes on, but none of them matched this likeness. It was an odd descriptor, but it was within the realm of both possibility and probability. A man would have to be larger than Mr. Wickham to have overpowered him in order to get him to take the pill that killed him. The square-toed shoes were obvious, as was the cigar. Through observing the crime scene, if one looked closely enough, there were footprints on the floors matching a square toed boot and there were ashes that could only have come from a cigar. I did not know how Mr. Holmes came to the conclusion that his feet were disproportionate to his body, though my assumption was that the footprints combined with the fact that Mr. Wickham had to have been killed by someone larger than himself allowed him to deduce the height and size of his feet, and the fact that they were not proportionate.

Lydia was still resting when we broke our fast in the morning. She had been through an ordeal and needed her rest more than any of us. It was here that Mr. Bingley broke the news he would be moving as soon as this business was dealt with.

"I shall be leaving Netherfield Park once we bring the man who committed this act to justice. I cannot in good conscience remain here, under this roof, knowing what has taken place."

"Rightly so, I could not abide by it, dear brother," Caroline Bingley replied.

By all appearances, Miss Bingley seemed to be less shaken than the rest of us about the murder. Mr. Holmes had clearly not gotten a wink of sleep, which made me feel guilty for getting hours of good rest. I had been exhausted by the previous day and despite the horrifying events, I was able to sleep soundly and for many hours. I knew it was not the violence of the events that kept Mr. Holmes awake, however. He was consumed by the case, running it over in his mind, trying to discover who the killer was from simple observations and Lydia's detailing of the events.

"I understand why you must go, but we shall all mourn you after you depart," Jane said softly.

The candidness of her statement took us all aback. It was very forward of her to say such a thing. Mr. Bingley turned to look at Jane and agreed that he would mourn their parting as well. The death of Mr. Wickham seemed to give them the ability to speak their minds in a way they were fearful to do before. Miss Bingley looked aghast at their confessions, but remained quiet. Mama, though she was still consumed with worry for Lydia, near burst into tears at Jane's and Mr. Bingley's statements. Whether they were tears of happiness that the two had finally made their feelings for one another clear or with sadness that Mr. Bingley should be leaving shortly, I do not know.

"When shall you depart?" Papa asked sullenly.

"I would not feel right to depart until after the case is solved, so that should depend on Mr. Holmes."

Mr. Holmes calmly answered, "I shall have the truth discovered in just a short while. I am close to cracking it now."

I peered at Mr. Holmes over the top of my glass, unsure whether he was fibbing to put everyone at ease or if he truly believed he would be able to solve the case within a short time.

It was unorthodox, but Mr. Bingley extended our welcome until Lydia seemed to be strong enough to leave with us. She had been shaken by the events more than we originally thought and had been unable to get out of her bed since her head hit the pillow the night before. It was as though Mr. Bingley felt responsible because Mr. Wickham was killed under his roof, though I knew him to be innocent of any direct relation with the crime.

As we left breakfast, I went to confront Mr. Holmes. He knew more about Mr. Wickham than the rest of us and I needed to know what it was he knew about the man. I also needed to know if he had been bluffing about being close to solving the case in order to quell anxieties.

"Mr. Holmes, are you really close to figuring out who the murderer was?"

"Oh, I already know."

"You could not possibly know already."

He smiled at me, that same mischievous glimmer in his eyes and I knew that what he said was the truth.

"Then why have you not apprehended the man yet?" I said. Although I had not been in the world of crime solving for long, I was quite certain that the apprehension of the culprit was an important part of the process.

"Well, Miss Bennet, I have not apprehended him yet, because the true killer was not a man."

I balked at this. Both sexes were, of course, capable of violence, but it would be rather unheard of for a woman to kill a man in cold blood. I was also sure that I would recall if I had seen a woman of six feet at the ball.

"How is that possible? By your own description of the assailant, it can't possibly be a woman."

Mr. Holmes nodded. "Well, yes."

"So your description was inaccurate?"

He scoffed at the very notion. "No. Not in the slightest."

Mr. Holmes had lost me. I was sure he had gone insane at some point during the night as there was no way his description could be accurate and the assailant could be a woman. The two negated one another, yet he was insisting both to be true.

He gazed at my puzzled expression for a moment before launching into his explanation. "Well, it was a man and a woman to be more accurate. A woman paid our six-foot-tall attacker to kill Mr. Wickham. This was a hired hit. And the woman who hired him is still under this roof. She will lead us to her hired man."

"A woman under this roof committed this murder?" I asked, a dreadful feeling in my stomach rising up. "Even though she is a woman, why have you not taken her into custody?"

"Because I cannot yet prove motive."

"What more motive do you require? We have revenge in blood on the wall and by Lydia's account of Mr. Wickham's behavior towards her, it is not difficult to see what a woman might want revenge against the wicked man for."

"I believe that RACHE was a diversion, something the murderer wrote on the wall to keep us distracted and keep our focus away from the true murderer, which would be the woman who paid to have Mr. Wickham killed."

"You clearly believe you know who it is. Will you tell me, sir?"

I had my own suspicions based off of his theory. No one in my family could possibly be a suspect. None of us had known Mr. Wickham long enough to have enough rage against him to do such a thing, nor did we possess the funds and the means to hire a killer. That left only Mr. Bingley's sisters.

"I discovered a ring on the floor underneath the body, as though it were a calling card of some kind. It told me who must be the killer."

He again ignored my request to know which woman hired the assailant. He was a theatrical man and would not reveal his climax before it was time.

"The ring is petite. It is not a wedding band, but rather a piece of jewelry meant to accessorize, to flaunt, which tells me that the offending woman was fairly well off. You and your family are clearly not suspects." He meant this in a reassuring manner, but I could not help but take some offense at the statement. "Which leaves only the Bingley sisters. I have known them both well for a while now, and I believe them both to be capable of something like this. I have yet to discover what either of them should gain from Mr. Wickham's death." He was clearly upset that he could not figure out this piece of the puzzle for himself.

Rather than continuing on this subject, I stated, "I would like to know about what happened between yourself and Mr. Wickham in the past." This had been biting at me for a long while now and though I did not think it relevant to solving the case, I was not requesting that he speak to the nature of their relationship, I was telling him to.

"It has no pertinence to this case, but I shall tell you regardless. I do not believe you have given me a choice in the matter. I was hired to find Mr. Wickham by a wealthy gentleman. Mr. Wickham had taken his younger sister, Georgiana Darcy, a girl of but fifteen, just like your Lydia, with the promise to wed her. He doubled back on his promise as soon as he discovered that he would not be able to touch her rather large inheritance, leaving the girl heartbroken. The man hired me to find Mr. Wickham so that he would remain quiet about the situation, saving the poor girl's reputation. It was different from my normal sort of work, but I took the job anyway.

"The really terrible part is that the gentleman who hired me, his father practically raised Mr.

Wickham as his own and left him some money after he died. Mr. Wickham lost it all to gambling, women, and libation. It was only when this ran out that he returned and manipulated the young girl into running away with him. Although he denied it, and apparently does still to this day, he accepted the hush money without question and I had not seen him since, until the other day on the way to town. That was how I met Mr. Bingley, actually. He is the closest companion of the gentleman who hired me. He aided me in the search for Mr. Wickham."

My mind raced following the story and suddenly, I had an idea. "Were either of Mr. Bingley's sisters involved in the search, or at the very least knew what was happening?"

"Neither were a part of the search, but I believe that both knew the story. Miss Bingley cared for the young girl once we got her back. She did not leave her side for many days. The girl was shaken and heartbroken, worried about her reputation and shaming the family. She was much like Lydia in many ways, both take hardship similarly in the inability to rise from bed or stop weeping."

"That is your motive, sir," I said without hesitation. I knew that should Mr. Wickham have left Lydia in this same state and not have been dead, I would have wanted to hire someone to kill him, as well. It was a ghastly thing to think, and I would not have admitted it out loud, but it was the truth. I felt a fierce protectiveness over Lydia and all my other sisters. Should someone hurt them, I would want to hurt the one who brought them pain.

"What is?" he asked, looking genuinely perplexed. It seemed as though the man had no concept of the relationships people share and how those can motivate even the kindest souls to do the darkest deeds.

"Miss Bingley wanted Mr. Wickham to pay for what he did to the young girl she cared about. She was tormented by the pain he caused and could not abide by it any longer. She did it out of love for the girl and hatred of Mr. Wickham."

Mr. Holmes lit up at my deduction. He may be good with observations of clues and inanimate objects, but my skill seemed to lie in the observation and understanding of human nature.

"You are not incorrect, Miss Bennet," Miss Bingley said coolly, making me jump.

Mr. Holmes' smile faltered as she stepped forward from the shadows of the doorway in which she'd been lurking. I did not know how much she had heard of our conversation, but surely it was enough.

"But that was not my only reasoning for hiring a man to kill Mr. Wickham." She spoke calmly and softly, as though she knew she would eventually be discovered before she had even committed the act.

"What was your other motivation?" Mr. Holmes asked.

I could feel my heartbeat through my whole body and my blood rush in my veins.

He added, "And why leave the ring?"

Mr. Holmes' curiosity was as palpable as my own. There was not a question that could be asked that we were uninterested in hearing the answer to.

"The ring was not purposeful. The plan was to get Mr. Wickham alone and distract him, but he had plans of his own. When I saw him steal away with Lydia, it only solidified my resolve to see him dead. I seduced Mr. Wickham after I heard Lydia run out crying. It was not hard, as the man will accept any partner, willing or otherwise. I would not let him do to another girl what he did to Georgiana. I suppose at some point, he pulled the ring from my finger, though I did not notice it. Add pickpocket to the list of crimes Mr. Wickham committed without answering to.

"I hired a man named Mr. Hope to kill him. While I distracted Mr. Wickham, Mr. Hope crept into the room and made sure he was cornered. He had no trouble with this, as Mr. Wickham was intimidated by a man larger than himself. Mr. Hope has a specific methodology that I could not make him sway from. The man, I assume to quell his own religious guilt, gives his victims a choice between two pills. One pill is harmless. The other contains a poison that will render the victim unconscious in seconds and dead within minutes. Mr. Hope said that whichever pill was chosen would then be the will of God. Mr. Wickham chose the poisoned pill, so evidently, it was the will of God that he is dead."

She ended her speech in a tone of vindictive spite that was almost tangible and harsh enough that I would believe it capable of slicing through steel.

"You have not given your other reason, sister," Mr. Bingley said, making the three of us jump.

As we turned, we discovered that not just he, but Papa and Jane had heard the entirety of Miss Bingley's hateful speech. Mr. Bingley had tears welling in his eyes, unable to stop them from pouring over.

"Charles," Miss Bingley gasped. In contrast to her harsh tone, her brother's name came out as a mere whisper, barely a breath.

"What was your other motivation?" Mr. Bingley demanded, raising his voice for what I imagine to be the first time in his life.

"Her." Miss Bingley pointed towards Jane. "I could not have you marrying so below your rank. I knew that should something like Mr. Wickham's death occur here and in such a public manner, you would no longer want to stay. It is not just their status that is so far below us, dear brother, but her family has shown such impropriety over our time in knowing them. I know it to be an advantageous match, and Mrs. Bennet has been speaking of your non-existent engagement for weeks now. I should not think that Miss Bennet's feelings for you are genuine." Miss Bingley lost her vehemence in this speech. The fear of repercussions guided her now, and she shied away from her brother's sharp gaze.

"My feelings are more genuine than you would ever know." To my surprise, it was Jane who responded to Miss Bingley's accusation. She had an anger in her that I had not seen before. "I care for your brother more than I have cared for any man in my life, and he cares for me. Do not blame your murder of Mr. Wickham on your perception of mine and your brother's feelings for one another." I had never heard such a speech from Jane. Even half that would have been more hateful than she had ever previously been.

"I am sorry, Charles. I simply could not allow it."

"Thankfully, you are not in charge of me, *dear* sister," he replied.

Miss Bingley dissolved into tears and placed herself on one of the seats in the room.

"I am sorry to say it, but we will have to tell the detectives from Scotland Yard what has happened and what Miss Bingley has done," I said delicately.

Mr. Bingley nodded. He seemed shell-shocked, unable to pause the tears that streamed down his face. He was clearly sad for the loss of his sister.

In truth, Miss Bingley had ended not only Mr. Wickham's life that night, but her own, as well.

Chapter Seven:
The Truth Of The Matter

It was not much longer before the detectives from Scotland Yard came. With Miss Bingley's confession, which had been heard by many more than just a single witness, the case was closed with no further investigation. Whether they would have continued investigating and come to the same conclusion as Mr. Holmes did, should she not have confessed, I do not know, but I doubt that anyone should have been convicted of the murder. If they had convicted anyone, it would have ended up being no more than just a patsy.

Miss Bingley gave up the location of Mr. Hope with ease. They offered her a lesser sentence should she continue to aid the investigation instead of impeding it. Mr. Hope, it turned out, was wanted for multiple murders all over London. He always killed in the same manner and left the same message in blood on the wall for investigators to muddle over.

He had been paid well over the years to kill people for many others. It was a horrible business and I could scarcely believe that there was such high demand for it, but the number of so-called jobs that Mr. Hope had completed was immense. He maintained his innocence, however. He admitted to setting up the murders and accepting money in return for killing, but he truly did not see himself as a murderer. He believed that what he had done was simply move along the will of God. By giving the men he killed a choice between the poisoned pill and the harmless pill, he claimed he had no responsibility if the pill consumed led them to their demise. According to Mr. Holmes, he was suffering from a delusion that caused him to believe that what he had done would not be considered murder, but be considered right and just.

Mr. Bingley still chose to leave Netherfield Park and return to his home in London. Netherfield Park had begun as a haven from the depravity of the city, but it had become a place full of memories the poor man would rather forget.

The death of Mr. Wickham had sparked something in both himself and Jane, though. They both must have felt the pressure of how short life can truly be. They were shy and retiring people, but neither wanted to lose the other. Should Mr. Bingley lose more than his sister as a result of the murder of Mr. Wickham, then I believe he would become a broken, shell of a man. The addition of Mr. Bingley's imminent departure to Jane's and Mr. Bingley's newly confessed love prompted Mr. Bingley to ask Jane to be his wife. I had never seen a woman so happy and should she know more happiness than that, I would be convinced that it should kill her. The only one who could have been known to be happier than Mr. Bingley and Jane at the news of their engagement was Mama.

Mr. Holmes had returned to London with the detectives from Scotland Yard. A new case had begun that they needed assistance on. Mr. Holmes was not keen on the idea of assisting them yet again. In the case of Mr. Wickham, he had simply needed to, as there were no other detectives present to help. I had discovered his usual clients were people who came to visit him in his apartment, private cases. It was rare that he was a consulting detective on an official case. He complained that he would not get credit for solving the case, that the only names to show up in the newspapers would be official policemen and detectives.

I could understand the desire he had for notoriety. He deserved it, but I did not believe he could stay away from a case for the simple reason of vanity. I knew he would take near every case that came his way, if only to prove to himself that he was clever enough to solve it.

I felt the loss of his presence. Lydia was still mending and with her taking up all of Mama's attention, I was able to go about my day almost completely freely. She was more concerned with Lydia's health than with marrying any of her daughters off, at least for the moment. I could not help but feel boredom creep into my daily routine again. The only people I encountered on a regular basis were those that I had known my whole life. I had very little new to learn about them, so my skills in observation were beginning to stagnate. I did not see a way out of these doldrums; they should surely be my own demise. I had developed a fondness for crime solving, deduction, and observation. Without them in my life I had begun to feel an unbearable emptiness.

With Jane gone and Mama tending to Lydia, the house was far too quiet. Kitty spent her days with Lydia, telling her stories and attempting to make her laugh again. Mary continued to practice her piano forte and was improving her talent with every new day. It was just I who felt lost now. I had found my talent and where I belonged, but it was not somewhere a woman was meant to be. Papa could not stand to see me so forlorn. He did everything in his power to raise my spirits, but he could not.

One dewy morning, Papa and I took a stroll through the gardens. After a few silent minutes, he turned to me.

"My dear Lizzy, I had a thought." He smiled mischievously at me. "What if you were to spend some time with Jane and Mr. Bingley in London?"

The true reason for a trip to London was not lost on me. If I went to visit Jane and Mr. Bingley, I could find Mr. Holmes.

So, to London I went, where I would help Mr. Holmes solve his cases and document the most intriguing ones we worked on together. This would be my happily ever after. A partnership of minds, not of marriage, would be my true way to happiness.

THE END

About the Author

Amelia works as a librarian and lives in an idyllic Cotswold village in England with Darcy, her Persian cat. She has been a Jane Austen fan since childhood but only in later life did she discover the glory and gory of a cozy mystery book. She has drafted many different cases for Holmes and Bennet to solve together.

Visit www.amelialittlewood.com for more details

KEEP READING...

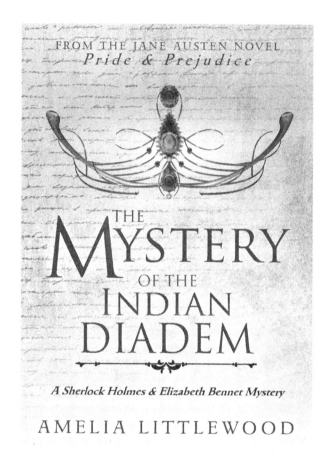

FROM THE JANE AUSTEN NOVEL
Pride & Prejudice

THE MYSTERY OF THE INDIAN DIADEM

A Sherlock Holmes & Elizabeth Bennet Mystery

AMELIA LITTLEWOOD

ELIZABETH BENNET GOES TO LONDON TO JOIN FORCES WITH SHERLOCK HOLMES ONCE AGAIN AND INVESTIGATE WHAT FIRST APPEARS TO BE AN ACCIDENTAL DEATH.

CYANIDE PUBLISHING

.

Made in United States
Orlando, FL
13 February 2025

58515100R00052